Herb Fairies
A Magical Tale of Plants & Their Remedies

When four young friends discover an herb fairy at the park, they are drawn into an adventure beyond their wildest dreams. The Old Man of the Forest has cast a terrible spell, locking up much of the plant magic in the world. The Herb Fairies turn to the children for help, and everyone discovers that the only way to restore the magic is by working together. By the end of this thirteen book series, readers become keepers of plant medicine magic.

Join the Herb Fairies Book Club!

Herb Fairies is a complete herbal learning system for kids.
For each of the thirteen books in the Herb Fairies series...

Draw and write about what you learned in your very own Magic Keeper's Journal.	Make the herbal remedies and recipes the kids make in the books with Recipe Cards!	Learn with puzzles, stories, songs, recipes, poems and games in Herbal Roots zine.	Color your favorite fairies or print out posters to hang on your bedroom wall.

Book club membership gives you access to the complete learning system on our mobile optimized site. Also includes audio books read by Kimberly, printable books and eBook versions for Kindle, iPad and other devices.

Visit **HerbFairies.com**

LearningHerbs

Herb Fairies
Book Eleven: Fireside Stories

Written by Kimberly Gallagher
Illustrated by Swapan Debnath
Produced by John M. Gallagher

If you are not sure what a word means or how it is pronounced, check the glossary in the back of the book.

Special Thanks to my mom, Cheryl Delmonte, a fellow writer, who has always encouraged my love for the craft of weaving stories for others to enjoy.

Special Thanks to Maryann Gallagher Agostin, Hailey Gallagher, Rowan Gallagher, Rosalee de la Forêt, and the LearningHerbs community.

ISBN: 978-1-938419-37-9

Published by LearningHerbs.com, LLC, Shelton, WA.
LearningHerbs and Herb Fairies logos are registered trademarks of LearningHerbs.com, LLC.
Herb Fairies is a registered trademark of LearningHerbs.com, LLC.
First print edition, January 2017. Published and printed in the U.S.A. on FSC® certified paper.

The Herb Fairies series is dedicated to the memory of
James Joseph Gallagher, Sr.

For Rowan and Hailey...

CHAPTER 1
A Spooky Tale?

Rowan was anxiously awaiting his turn as the storyteller. Camie and Hailey's wilderness school class and their families and friends were gathered around a fire in a circular canvas hut. They were sharing stories and songs. Rowan, Camie, and Hailey were all excited that their friend Sarah had come along too. She wasn't in wilderness school, but ever since they'd started having adventures together in the Fairy Herb Garden the four had become inseparable. Rowan knew Sarah would love his story. It was so spooky.

It was snowing gently outside, but between the fire and the warmth of everyone's bodies it was cozy in the hut. Everyone was focused on Natalie, one of the wilderness school instructors, as she wove one of her favorite tales. This one was about a hare whose coat had changed so he could easily blend into the winter landscape. Rowan knew he would be telling his story when Natalie finished. He loved telling stories in the firelight, and he was thinking of ways he could make the story even spookier.

That's when it happened. Suddenly, Rowan got a flash in his mind of his little sister Hailey and her friends trying to go to sleep that night. Their eyes were wide with fear, and they were holding hands. Some even looked like they had tears in their eyes. Just after this image flashed in his mind, Rowan felt something drop into his coat pocket.

He was reminded of a similar moment about a month ago when he and his friends had first encountered a brownie. Brownies, it turned out, were small, magical, brown beings who moved through the mists helping people treat each other better. They helped people by offering flashes of insight like the one Rowan had just experienced. He realized that with so many little kids present, it would be better to choose a different story. Especially since Hailey's class was planning to sleep up here in the hut tonight. For some of them it might even be their first time sleeping in the wilderness.

Rowan carefully opened his pocket and peered inside. Sure enough, there was a tiny woman in there. Like the other brownie they'd met, she was dressed in short brown pants that came to her knees. She wore a billowy pink shirt and a long brown coat with a matching brown hat. She had large pointy ears that stuck out from her head, large round eyes and a long nose.

She was completely passed out. Rowan remembered how the first brownie, Compassion, had explained that brownies didn't usually fall through the mists. Rowan knew this must be another one of the brownie magic keepers. He and his friends were helping to heal the magic keepers from all the different magical races. All the magic keepers were really sick, and that's why the brownie magic keepers were accidentally falling through the mists when they tried to help people.

"Rowan...Rowan." Suddenly Rowan was aware that someone was calling his name. He looked up. "It's your turn," Natalie said.

Rowan thought fast. He knew he couldn't tell the story he'd been planning to tell, and he also knew that he had to help this brownie as quickly as possible. She was not in good shape. "Um. Can we take a bathroom break first?" he asked. "I've got to go."

"Do other people need a bathroom break?" Natalie asked.

Rowan poked Hailey. "Raise your hand," he whispered urgently, pointing to his pocket. Hailey could see by the way Rowan was looking at her that something important was happening. She raised her hand and Rowan pulled his pocket open so she could peek inside. When she saw the brownie, Hailey squealed with delight.

"Brownie," she whispered to Camie, who was sitting next to her. Camie's hand immediately shot into the air, and Sarah's too. Hailey saw that Rowan had told her.

Several other hands were up as well, and Natalie agreed to let people go outside for a few minutes. One mom was taking some of the kids down to the honey bucket, so Rowan knew they'd have at least a little bit of time before anyone missed them. Rowan slipped his backpack over his shoulder and headed outside with the others. The four friends gathered together outside the hut. They pulled their coats tightly around them. It was super cold in the snow. "We've got to call the mists," said Rowan. "This brownie needs to get to Fairy Herb Garden fast."

"It's lucky we're already on wilderness school land," said Sarah. "This is where we called the mists last time."

"Let's go into the trees a bit, so no one sees us disappear," said Camie.

"Everybody hold hands," said Hailey when they'd found a good place in a little grove of cedars.

"And don't let go!" Sarah reminded them.

The four friends focused their attention on the Fairy Herb Garden. They called to mind the faces of some of their friends there—Melissa, the lemon balm fairy; Tago, the plantain fairy; Stellaria, the chickweed fairy; and Dandy, the dandelion fairy. They pictured Cally's courtyard calendula home where they'd met and healed one of the elf magic keepers, and the fountain where the fairies left their gift for the May Queen each spring. The garden had become one of their favorite places, and it was fun to picture it in such detail. They held the image in their minds even as they opened their eyes to check for the mists.

It looked as if a thick fog was rolling toward them over the snow. The four friends held tight to each other's hands and stepped forward to meet it. As the mists enveloped them the chill in the air became even more intense, and everywhere they looked it was the same deep grey. They held tight to each other's hands and began to focus their attention on individual fairies, remembering that it was the fairies who had pulled them through the mists the last time.

Suddenly, Rowan had another thought. The fairies had pulled them through, but the brownie had helped too. He had used the last of his strength to get them through the mists. *What if they couldn't do it without a brownie helping?* Rowan felt panic begin to rise in him. The mists seemed to be pressing on him and it seemed like the feeling would never end. This was much scarier than his story was going to be. He felt terrified that they were going to be lost in the mists forever. He couldn't even see his friends, the fog was so thick around him. Then he felt his little sister's

hand in his. It was the only warmth in this sea of cold. *I have to get Hailey through*, he thought. He focused all his energy on Strobus, the pine fairy they'd met on their last adventure. He was an old, wise Native American tree fairy, and Rowan knew he would be able to pull them through.

He felt Strobus first, but then there were Dandy and Melissa, Miles and Viola, and all of the many fairies they'd met, and even some they didn't know. The fairies were pulling the children forward, out of the mists. It was such a strange feeling, moving forward even when their legs were completely still. The moment they broke free of the mists, the chill was so intense, took their breath away, and the children stumbled forward, falling to the ground dizzy and shaken.

CHAPTER 2
Rose Hip Healing

Dandy flew over them, sprinkling them with fairy dust. As the golden powder settled on their skin, the dizziness cleared from their heads and the children felt the familiar tingling sensation that accompanied their shrinking to fairy size. Soon they were surrounded by fairies helping them to their feet and hugging them in relief and welcome.

"We've got to find a better way for you to get to the herb garden," said Strobus finally. "I'm guessing you found another brownie."

Rowan nodded and reached into his pocket to retrieve the little brown woman. She was extremely tiny now, since the fairy dust had shrunk her right along with the children. As he lifted her up, Rowan noticed that she was burning hot. "I think she's got a fever," he said. Then he noticed the blood. The side of her pants was ripped and she had a gash across her thigh. "Oh, she's wounded too! I hope I didn't hurt her somehow."

"We should get her someplace warm," said Sarah, putting a reassuring hand on Rowan's shoulder.

"Come with me." A confident, strikingly beautiful Chinese fairy stepped forward, introducing herself as Rosa. She wore a pink dress made of overlapping rose petals, and her silky black hair was pinned up on her head and decorated with a rose flower. Her face had a delicate beauty, but there was a sharpness to her eyes and the children noticed that her fingernails were filed into points. Her golden wings were made up of oval, toothed leaflets coming to delicate points at their tips.

"I have just the thing for that wound," she said, "and I've already got a fire going."

Hailey stepped forward happily, breathing in the wonderful scent that accompanied this fairy. She knew without a doubt that this was the rose fairy, and was sure she could help them make a rose hip poultice for the wound. It would be the perfect medicine this time of year.

The others were a little more hesitant, the fairy's eyes and fingernails giving them pause, but they'd learned to trust Hailey's intuition, and they followed their friend. "Her fingernails look a little scary," Camie whispered to Hailey.

"Oh, they're just like the thorns on the rose plants," Hailey whispered back. "Don't worry. Rose is an incredibly healing plant," she said reassuringly.

Before long, the children were making their way carefully through the thorny stems of a rosebush. Incredibly, this plant had green leaves even though it was January. The children knew this must be the fairy's home. All the other rosebushes around it were bare except for the bright red rose hips that still decorated some of their stems. Each fairy used magic to keep the plants that made up their homes green and growing all year round. Most of the plants in the Fairy Herb Garden followed the same cycles as plants everywhere, dying back in the winter, sprouting in the spring, blossoming in summer, and seeding in the fall.

Rosa welcomed them into a cozy living room. She did have a fire going inside a wood stove in the corner of the room. The stove had a long chimney and the children imagined it reaching upward all the way to the top of the rosebush, some three feet from the ground, so the smoke could make it to open air. The fairy's living room was decorated in beautiful shades of pink. There was a twig couch with a rose petal stuffed cushion on it. A soft pink blanket was draped over the cushion. She had the most amazing chairs. They looked like rose petals sitting on the ground, but they were firm when you sat down. You could rock a bit as you sat around the white rug decorated with roses. A small table next to the couch held a vase filled with blooming wild roses. The scent from the flowers drifted through the air, reminding everyone of the sweetness of spring.

"Why don't you lay the brownie on the couch," said Rosa, spreading a white towel over part of the pink blanket. "Then I can restore her to her proper size and we can get a good look at that wound."

Rowan laid the brownie gently on the couch. As he let go of her, the brownie's eyes opened a little bit, and she looked around deliriously, eyes wide and panicked. "Where am I?" she asked in a tiny, frightened voice.

Sarah stepped forward and knelt next to the couch. "Don't be scared. You're in the Fairy Herb Garden," she said in her soothing voice that had calmed so many magic keepers before. "You fell through the mists, and you're pretty sick, but we can help you."

The brownie looked up into Sarah's kind eyes and fainted.

"Let's get her back to her right size," said Sarah, and Rosa flew over the couch, sprinkling fairy dust on the brownie. She grew to her normal size, which was still only about two inches tall, much smaller than the five-inch fairies.

The children gathered around her, peering at the wound on her leg. Camie looked away quickly. The wound was full of puss and yellow with bright red around it, and it smelled bad.

"This wound is infected," said Hailey. "It can't have come from anything you did," she added, looking at Rowan. "I think maybe it just started bleeding again because it rubbed up against your pocket. She's had it for a while if it looks like this. Rosa, you said you had something to help with it?"

Rosa nodded and flew into the kitchen. She returned with her mortar and pestle and four acorn cups filled with tea. "I've brought you some rose hip tea," she said, flying to Camie first. Camie took the cup gratefully. The sight of that wound had been a bit too much for her, and she had collapsed into a rose petal chair, taking deep breaths of the rose-scented air. Rosa put the tray of cups on the table next to the flower vase, and flew the mortar and pestle over to Hailey.

As Hailey had guessed, there were rose hips inside, seeded and ready to be crushed into a poultice.

"What's in there?" Sarah asked curiously. She loved learning about plant medicine.

Hailey held the mortar and pestle so Sarah could see inside. "They're rose hips," she explained. "So we can make a poultice."

"What are rose hips?" asked Sarah. "I've never heard of them."

"They're the fruits of the rose plant," Rowan explained.

Hailey had begun mashing them up with the pestle.

"I never knew rose plants made fruit," said Sarah.

"Would you like to taste one?" Rosa asked. The tray with the tea cups was decorated with roses and their hips.

"Are they good?" Sarah asked hesitantly.

"Delicious!" said Rowan, taking one from the tray. "Just eat the outside," he instructed. "The seeds are not good for you." Rowan found that this was much easier to do when he was fairy sized. He got a mouthful easily, and smiled at the zingy, citrus taste.

Sarah took a bite as well. "Wow! Those are good. They remind me of oranges, somehow."

"They're full of vitamin C, just like oranges," said Rowan. "They're great for you when you're sick."

"I bet the tea is delicious too," said Sarah, picking up a cup and looking over at Camie.

"It is," said Camie. She smiled, feeling much better with the warm liquid in her stomach.

Hailey had finished mashing up the poultice and started spreading it on the brownie's leg wound.

"Oh, ouch!" the brownie yelped, her eyes flying open. "What are you doing? Where am I? Who are you?"

Rosa saw the panic in the brownie's eyes and had an idea. She flew quickly to her medicine chest, and was back in a flash. Sarah was kneeling next to the brownie again, speaking softly to her, but the panic was not receding.

Rosa dropped a few drops of tincture into the brownie's mouth. At first it looked like the brownie was going to spit

it back out, but then she took a deep, shuddery breath and closed her eyes. When she opened them again the panic had left her eyes and she was able to focus on the room around her.

"What did you give her?" Hailey asked.

"A rose tincture I make every year," said Rosa. "It's made with rose petals, leaves, and bark, and it's very calming. Great for trauma."

"It sure is!" said Camie from her chair. She was amazed at how fast the tincture had calmed the brownie down.

CHAPTER 3
Learning to Look Closely

"Hey," said the brownie, "I think I'm remembering something...some kind of riddle."

The children leaned in closer to the brownie, eager to hear the riddle. They knew it would help them to guess the brownie's name and help restore the rose magic. Already they'd healed troll, elf, and dwarf magic keepers and this was the second brownie they'd found. If they could find one more, they could restore all of the plant magic!

"My name happens in moments that are quiet and still." The brownie paused. "That's odd," she said. "A riddle about my name, but of course I already know my name..." As she said it, the brownie's face went through a series of expressions, ending in disbelief.

"It's okay," Sarah said soothingly. "We've helped lots of other magic keepers remember their names. We can help you too."

"Magic keepers?" the brownie asked. She was no longer panicked, but she was very confused. "Did I fall through the mists again?" she asked. "Who are you children, and why are you so small?"

Sarah explained how the brownie had fallen into Rowan's pocket, and how they had brought her to the Fairy Herb Garden because they'd found the healing goes much quicker here than anywhere else. She also explained how they'd found and healed another brownie named Compassion just the month before.

At this piece of news the brownie sat up excitedly, but she quickly fell back down onto the bed. "Oh, my head hurts," she said. "And my throat is so sore. I think I have a fever too. I guess I'm lucky I dropped into your pocket, huh, Rowan?"

"Very lucky!" Rowan agreed. "My sister Hailey is really great with the plants. If anyone can heal you, she can."

Hailey smiled at Rowan's praise. "Is it okay if I finish putting this poultice on your leg wound?" Hailey asked. "It's very infected, and this will help a lot."

"Yes," said the brownie sheepishly. "I'm sorry I pulled away before, but it did hurt when you put it on."

"It'll only hurt for a minute," Sarah reassured her, "and then you'll feel so much better." Sarah stepped forward and helped Hailey smooth the rose hip poultice onto the infected wound. They worked as gently as they could, but still the brownie winced in pain as it was applied.

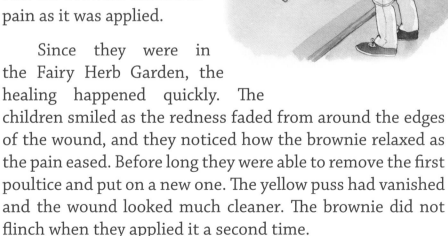

Since they were in the Fairy Herb Garden, the healing happened quickly. The children smiled as the redness faded from around the edges of the wound, and they noticed how the brownie relaxed as the pain eased. Before long they were able to remove the first poultice and put on a new one. The yellow puss had vanished and the wound looked much cleaner. The brownie did not flinch when they applied it a second time.

While they were waiting for the poultice to do its work Sarah put her hand on the brownie's forehead. "You've definitely got a fever," she said. "Hailey, can roses help with the flu?"

"As a matter of fact, one of our family's favorite remedies for the flu is a tea made from rose hips, elderflowers, yarrow, and mint. Rosa, do you have those things?"

"I've definitely got the rose hips, but I think we'll have to visit some other fairy homes to get those other ingredients."

"I'll go," said Camie, always up for adventure. "I remember where the elder tree is. I'd love to see Cerulea again, and I think there was yarrow growing near the elder. I'm sure Cerulea can help me find Piper or Spica so I can get some mint."

"I'll come with you," said Rowan. "To help you carry everything."

Hailey was glad Rowan was going with Camie. She knew her friend loved adventure, but sometimes Camie overestimated her ability to find her way. Hailey knew that Rowan would be able to help if she got lost.

By the time Sarah and Hailey removed the second poultice from the brownie's leg wound, new pink skin had already started to grow.

"Wow!" said the brownie, gently touching the healed wound with her finger. "That's been sore for a long, long time. It feels great. Thank you so much!" With that pain relieved, the brownie lay back and fell into a restful, though fevered, sleep.

Rosa settled delicately into her rocking chair and smiled at the girls as Sarah pulled out her sketch book and began to draw the rose plant. They were waiting for Rowan and Camie to return with the tea ingredients. It was great that magic kept Rosa's rugosa rose house green and growing even in January. Hailey was able to show Sarah how each leaf on the rugosa rose plant was actually made up of five to seven leaflets. She explained how rugosa actually means "wrinkled," like the rose plant's leaves. They also looked at the thorns on the rose stems. They looked incredibly big and sharp because the girls were so small.

The vase of flowers allowed Sarah to draw the petals correctly. She noticed that each of the wild rose flowers had five pink petals and a yellow center. She loved being close enough to draw them because she loved that rose petal smell.

Finally, Sarah drew the rose hips. "I can't believe I never noticed that rose plants even had fruit before," she said.

"Sometimes our eyes only see what they know to look for," said Rosa quietly. "But you children are learning to look closer. That is helping to bring the plant magic back as much as healing these magic keepers." Rosa had a cool, queenly way about her, but her smile showed how happy that thought made her.

CHAPTER 4
Achillea Offers to Help

Camie and Rowan moved carefully through the thorny opening of Rosa's home out into the Fairy Herb Garden. Camie looked around, trying to get her bearings, but nothing looked familiar in the moonlight. The shadows were long and the garden was eerily quiet. Snow fell gently, obscuring everything in a blanket of white.

"Look, Camie," Rowan whispered. "There's the very top of the maypole. Remember the fairies' spring festival?"

Camie looked where Rowan was pointing, and sure enough, she did see the top of the maypole. She smiled at Rowan. Now she had a sense of where they were. She knew Rosa's home was at the edge of the garden. She'd noticed the Enchanted Forest behind it when they had come earlier. Scanning back from the maypole along the edge of the garden, she saw the Scotch broom thicket where they had met Awareness, the troll. She knew that Cerulea's elder tree was at the opposite end of the garden from the maypole, so she turned to the right. She had to squint to see the far end of the garden in the moonlight, but then the elder tree came into focus. Its bare, grey branches were dusted with a light layer of snow, giving them a subtle glow.

"Come on," said Camie, "this way." She led Rowan down the garden path toward the elder tree.

Rowan smiled as Camie led the way. He was proud of her for taking her time and figuring out where they needed to go. The Fairy Herb Garden was very quiet as they walked through it. Snow was falling gently and most all of the plants had died back for the winter. There were small patches of green here and there where the fairies were maintaining their plant homes with the help of their magic. What fairies they saw seemed drowsy, even though it was only about seven o'clock in the evening. Camie was glad that Rowan had offered to go with her. She found the garden beautiful, but a bit spooky.

When they reached the elder tree, they noticed one area where the leaves were still green and growing, and when they looked closely they could see Cerulea's swing among the branches. Near the swing, they saw Cerulea herself, snuggled into her hammock, sleeping.

"Cerulea. Cerulea!" they called, but their voices came out hushed and tiny.

"Oh, we'll never wake her up this way," said Camie. "What should we do?"

"Hmmmm," said Rowan. "Didn't you say you thought there was a yarrow patch around here somewhere? Maybe the yarrow fairy will be at home and she can help us."

Camie looked around. The last time they'd been here it was warm and sunny, and all the plants were green and growing. She didn't recognize anything at first, but she took a deep breath and tried to remember where she'd seen that patch of yarrow. She'd been up on the swing when she'd noticed it, and she was swinging out away from where Cerulea was sleeping. She turned in the right direction and peered into the shadows. "There," she said triumphantly. "See, it's just ahead. That patch of green."

She and Rowan moved toward the spot carefully. There was no path here, so they had to walk with caution, climbing over rocks and tree roots. As they got closer, Rowan could see that Camie was right. There in front of them were the feathery leaves of a yarrow plant. They were tall and green, making him think that they must be part of a fairy home. Even though the yarrow in their garden stayed green all year, it wasn't usually this tall in the winter.

"Hello!" Camie called, walking around the plant, looking for some sort of entrance to the fairy's house.

"Hello!" Rowan called out too, following his friend.

"Hello?" A little fairy head suddenly popped out of the yarrow patch just in front of them, making them jump. "Oh, it's you," the fairy said, recognizing the children. "Why aren't you with Rosa and the brownie?"

"We needed some more herbs to help with her flu," Camie explained. "We were hoping you could help us out with some dried yarrow leaves and flowers."

"No problem," said the fairy. Her head disappeared for a moment, but soon she was back with a jar of dried yarrow for them. When she stepped out of her home, the children could see that she had the light skin of a European woman, and straight honey-blond hair. She wore a simple green dress with white and pink yarrow flowers in a band across the bottom of it. Her wings were feathery with deep cuts, like yarrow leaves. Her wand was a sprig of yarrow with three beautiful white umbels of yarrow flowers. Rowan always remembered that yarrow was good at stopping bleeding and helping heal deep cuts because of those deep cuts in the leaves of the plant. The fairy introduced herself as Achillea. She was very excited to finally be meeting the children. "I'm so glad I could help," she said.

"Thank you," said Camie. "Would you be willing to help us some more?" she asked. "You see, we need some elder flowers too, but Cerulea seems to be sleeping."

"Yes, most of the fairies are very sleepy this time of year. As our plants die back, we get more and more tired."

"You don't seem tired, though," Rowan pointed out.

"Well, yarrow plants don't completely die back in the winter, either," said Achillea. "I don't get as sleepy as the others, and luckily I know right where Cerulea keeps her dried flowers. I know she would want to help." Achillea flew up into Cerulea's tree house and came back with a jar of dried white elder flowers.

"Thank you again," said Camie. "Now we need some mint, but I don't think I've ever been to Piper's home. Does she live near Melissa, the lemon balm fairy?" Camie shivered a bit in the cold and wrapped her arms around herself. "Aren't you cold?" she asked Achillea, wondering how the fairy could stand to be outside in her short-sleeved flower dress and bare feet.

"Cold?" Achillea asked. "No. We fairies don't really get cold, or hot either. But you look cold."

Camie's teeth were chattering.

"Would you like me to fly over to Piper's and bring you some mint for the tea? I'd be happy to."

"That would be great," said Camie, eager to get back to the warm fire at Rosa's house.

"Good job finding Cerulea's house and finding the yarrow," said Rowan as they walked back to the rosebush, each carrying a jar of dried herbs. "You're going to be as good a tracker as me before long."

Camie smiled. She'd been practicing her tracking skills a lot at wilderness school, and loved these adventures with Rowan because she always learned things when they were together.

Achillea arrived at Rosa's shortly after Rowan and Camie. She carried two jars of mint leaves. "Spica insisted on sending some spearmint along as well," she explained. "Those two do most everything together. Their plants have even grown together. I found them curled up next to each other on their bed." The children smiled, remembering the spirited mint fairy sisters from their visit to Melissa's home.

Hailey already had water boiling for the tea, and they added the herbs they'd gathered to the pot with the rose hips. While it was steeping, the brownie awoke. "I've remembered another part to the riddle," she announced sleepily.

The children gathered round to listen. "My name begins with a prefix that means again, and ends the same as my brother's." The brownie's voice sounded raspy and they could tell that her throat was sore.

"Hmmmm," said Sarah. "I bet your name starts with re-. That's a prefix that means again."

"But who is your brother, and how would we know how his name ends?"

"You mentioned him earlier," said the brownie. "Compassion is my brother."

"Compassion!" said Hailey. "The brownie we healed last month. He's your brother?"

"Yes," said the brownie. "I hope I can find him soon. We usually work together, you see. That's part of why we're falling through the mists. We need each other to find our way safely. We need my other brother, too. I guess you haven't found him yet? I can't seem to remember his name..." The brownie looked very sad as she said this.

"We haven't found him yet," said Camie. "But I'm sure we will. He's the last magic keeper we need to heal!"

"I'm going to go ask Strobus if he knows where to find Compassion," said Achillea. "I'm sure he'll be eager to find you too." Achillea flew through Rosa's door and out into the garden.

"We still have to heal this brownie too," Hailey reminded them all, turning her attention back to the brownie. "We've got some tea to help with your flu. I bet it's steeped by now. Rosa, do you have any rose hip honey? I think that would be really good for the brownie's sore throat."

CHAPTER 5
A Happy Reunion

The brownie gratefully drank the cup of tea they offered, and smiled as she let the spoonful of rose hip honey melt in her mouth. "I think I might get sick more often. These things taste delicious!" she said. It wasn't long before the brownie's fever was gone, and her throat felt better. The plant medicine did its work quickly and efficiently.

"I remember the last part of the riddle," she said excitedly. "If you take time for this before you act, you may be able to avoid mistakes, and if you forget, practicing it can turn your most miserable failures into a shining success."

Hailey and Camie looked at each other with smiles on their faces. They'd figured out the riddle at the same moment. "We know this one!" they said.

Camie explained, "Our teacher at school is always reminding us to take time for..."

"Reflection!" The two girls said it together. They'd heard their teacher say it so many times, in just that same tone. He was always telling them how they could avoid making mistakes by taking the time for reflection, and they even had special time set aside each day before they went home to reflect about what they had learned.

"Reflection," said the brownie. "Reflection. Yes, that is my name. It does end the same as my brother's, doesn't it?"

"And it begins with re- like I thought it would," said Sarah, smiling at the little girls.

"And it happens in moments that are quiet and still," said Rowan. "Like the moment before I was going to tell that scary story to the little kids, and you fell into my pocket."

"We better get back soon. Everyone will be waiting for you to tell your story," said Camie.

"How much time do you think has passed in the human world while we've been here?" Rowan asked Rosa anxiously.

"We don't need to worry about that," said Reflection. "Brownies can move through time as easily as we move through space with the help of the mists. I can get you back in time to tell your story. Of course, it would be easier if my brothers were here…"

Reflection's voice trailed off, but Rowan's mind was still on the part about him telling his story. "I don't even know what story I'm going to tell," said Rowan.

"Hello?" A tiny voice was coming from the opening to Rosa's house. Everyone turned around to see who it was.

"Compassion!" Reflection was so excited at the sight of her brother that she ran to the door and swooped him up in a big hug.

Strobus and Achillea followed Compassion into the house. They both looked tired. "We called him from the mists," Strobus explained.

"I've been doing my best to work alone," said Compassion, "but it will be much easier now that we're together again." He smiled at his sister. "Have you released the rose magic yet?" he asked.

"The rose magic?" Reflection asked, and even as she said it, she began searching in the pockets of her coat.

Like Compassion's pockets, hers were filled with all sorts of treasures that fell to the floor when she turned them inside out. Tiny jelly beans fell from one. Another held all sorts of little plastic animals. A third was full of beautiful shells. But again, it wasn't until she found that pocket within a pocket  deep inside her coat that she pulled forth the leather pouch with no visible means of opening. "No zippers, no buttons, no snaps...not even a seam," she said quietly, tiredly. "I tried everything to get it open."

The children all nodded, having heard this story many times before. They recognized the sadness with which all the magic keepers spoke.

"I think I know how we can get the magic out," said Rowan, excited by his idea.

"How?" asked Hailey. She remembered how they had to go to Sean's house and return the book she'd taken from him in order to return the magic in Compassion's pouch.

"I bet we have to make up a story together," said Rowan. "A story I can tell instead of that scary one."

"Fun!" said Camie. "I love to make up stories."

"Do you think it will work?" Sarah asked Reflection. She'd noticed that magic keepers often had an intuition about how to release the magic once they were all gathered.

Reflection looked around at the fairies and the children, and she nodded slowly. "Yes," she said. "Yes, I do think it will work. That feels like just the right thing to do."

So everyone gathered around the fire, and Rosa brought out a special treat "to help your brains work creatively," she said. She handed each of them a bowl of rose hip pudding made with chia seeds.

"Oh my gosh!" said Camie. "This is delicious. I'm going to make some for my family as soon as we get home."

"How about if I start the story and then each of you add a part to it?" Rowan suggested. "We can just go around in a circle." Everyone agreed, and so Rowan began...

CHAPTER 6
A Story to Restore the Magic

"Once there was an elf named Shinaravna who lived in the Enchanted Forest near a village of trolls and not far from the Fairy Herb Garden. Shinaravna was a special elf. She was a magic keeper among her people. This meant that she was one of the elves responsible for keeping the magic alive in the world. Shinaravna was a young and playful elf, and in fact if you translated her name into our language it would be Play."

Hailey took the story from here and added, "Play knew the troll magic keepers well. Their names were Inspiration,

Awareness, and Trust. She was special friends with Awareness because he was a storyteller and a carver, and Play loved to listen to him tell the stories he had carved into his story sticks. Also, unlike most of the trolls, Awareness was comfortable in the forest and sometimes he and Play would go tracking together."

"One day while they were out tracking, they were very surprised to meet a dwarf," Camie added, bringing in the magical race she was most connected to. "Most dwarves stayed within dwarf mountain, digging tunnels and mining for precious gems, but this dwarf was one of the wanderers who traveled the world and collected stories to share with her people. The dwarf's name was Celebration, and they were excited to learn that she was also a magic keeper."

Strobus was next in the circle and spoke up, saying, "It is interesting that the three came together on this day of all days, because it was on this very day that the Old Man of the Forest finally lost his temper. The May Queen had been getting sicker and sicker as the plant magic faded more and more from the world."

"And the Old Man of the Forest loved the May Queen," said Rosa. "She was his guiding light. He could not stand to see her listless and ill. In his sadness and confusion, the Old

Man of the Forest blamed the fairies for the fading magic. He saw how they had stopped interacting with the humans, instead staying hidden among their plants.

He thought this was why humans were not coming to the plants for healing any longer, and why the magic had begun to fade."

"The Old Man of the Forest was unreasonably angry with the fairies and he cast a terrible spell," added Achillea. "He cast a spell that would take the plant magic away from the fairies forever."

"The three magic keepers were in the forest together when the spell was cast," said Compassion. "Shinaravna was just pointing out the deer tracks they'd been following so that Celebration could see them, when a darkness descended among the trees. All three companions put a hand to their heart. They could feel the magic being pulled away and it felt wrenchingly sad. They fell to their knees and covered their faces." As he spoke, everyone could see that he was remembering his own experience with that very day.

"Somewhere hidden within the mists, there were three brownies, a sister and her two brothers, who were also feeling that wrenching sadness," said Sarah, who could see that Reflection was in no shape to add to the story at that moment. The recently healed brownie was clutching her brother's hand and tears were streaming down her face. "The three held tight to each other. Their interlocked hands were their only grounding connection within the mists that allowed them to travel through time and space so they could help others in times of difficulty. It was the brownies that kept things flowing smoothly in the world. They helped people understand each other better,

and think before they acted foolishly, little things like that...little things that made all the difference."

"All the magic keepers felt it when the Old Man cast that terrible spell," said Reflection, finding her voice. "The other two dwarves back in the mountain felt it. The trolls in troll village felt it, and the elves in the forest felt it. The brownies were lucky in a way, that they were together when it happened." Everyone saw that she was noticing this for the first time as she added to the story. Tears still glistened in her eyes, and she squeezed her brother's hand a little tighter.

"Well," said Rowan. "The May Queen felt the impact of the spell as well. She knew she had to do something, and fast, or the magic truly would be lost forever. Using the last of her strength the May Queen cast a spell of her own. Her spell locked

up the plant magic and secured it with all of the different magic keepers. She sang her spell, and made a way that the magic could be restored if all of the different races worked together to release it."

Hailey spoke next. "The magic keepers tried everything to release the magic on their own. The trolls beat on the golden chests, even trying to split them open with axes, but nothing worked. The magic keepers became more and more upset, and eventually they began to get sick."

"The trolls scattered without the magic keepers to hold them together. The elves left the Enchanted Forest, seeking a healthier place to live," said Camie. "As for the May Queen, she fell into a deep slumber, and could not be awakened."

"The Old Man of the Forest, having used up his anger, realized his error, but it was too late. There was nothing he could do to reverse the spell." Strobus added this part.

"No one knew what to do," said Rosa. "The fairies were happy among their plants for a long time, but as time went by they began to feel drained of energy. They noticed their plants were becoming less and less healthy, and that their magic had faded."

"The fairies and the plants spoke to one another," said Achillea. "They came up with an idea. They knew that human children could sometimes still see fairies, and they thought that perhaps if they could connect with some human children, they might be able to help the plants and restore the magic."

Compassion and Reflection looked around at the circle of children and fairies. This was the first time they had heard this whole story, and they were obviously amazed by what they were discovering. Suddenly, all the pain and trouble they'd experienced was being explained. They felt incredibly grateful to the children for the part they were playing in healing all of the different magic keepers and bringing the plant magic back to the world. Neither of them spoke up to continue the story, so Sarah added the last few sentences.

"The fairies were able to find four children who were willing to help and one by one, with the help of the fairies, they used the plants to heal the magic keepers. Slowly but surely they worked to restore the magic to the world."

As she spoke these words, the little pouch in Reflection's hands began to glow and sparkle and then it split open and a bright pink glow filled the room, bringing with it the intoxicating scent of a rose garden. They had done it! The rose magic was restored. Rosa sparkled and glowed and she smiled a radiant smile at the children.

"Well," said Rowan. "I think you three are going to have to help me tell that story when we get back to the fire. Since we all made it up together."

The girls smiled, excited by the idea of sharing that particular story with their friends.

Reflection stepped forward then, for within the pouch she had found four round mirrors—one for each of the children. As she handed one to each of them she said, "These mirrors will help you remember me, since when you look in them you will see your own reflection, but also they will help you navigate the mists more easily next time. When you do find our brother, you'll be able to bring him back here without worrying about getting lost in the mists. Once you've called the mists, stand in a circle with the mirrors pointing toward one another and they will create an image of the Fairy Herb Garden, bringing you straight here. You'll be able to use them any time you want to, as long as you are all together."

The children looked at the tiny mirrors, and then smiled at one another. It felt good to know they could get back to the Fairy Herb Garden any time they wanted to. It was beginning to feel like a second home to them, and they loved their friends here very much.

"Now," said Strobus, "we'll send you back so you can share your story with your friends back home."

Rosa took out her fairy dust and sprinkled it over the children, causing them to tingle and grow back to their regular size while at the same time transporting them back to wilderness school land. As they emerged from among the trees, they could just hear Natalie's voice calling everyone back together to hear Rowan's story.

Glossary

Achillea (ă-kill-ee-ă): Name of the yarrow fairy and also the genus name of the yarrow plant.

Rosa (row-să): Name of the rose fairy and also the genus name of the rose plant.

Rugosa (rug-ō-să): species name of a wild rose plant.

What's Next?

Learn more about rose in the Herb Fairies member area!

After you complete the Magic Keeper's Journal, color Rosa, make some recipes, and print out a picture of her for your wall. Learn lots more about rose in Herbal Roots Zine, which has recipes, puzzles, activities, stories, songs and more!

Who's next? Meet... ⟶

Herb Fairies

Zeylani is the Cinnamon Fairy. Join him in

Book Twelve: Zeylani's Tropical Oasis.

Author Kimberly Gallagher, M.Ed. is also creator of *Wildcraft!, An Herbal Adventure Game*, by LearningHerbs.com. Her Masters in Education is from Antioch University in Seattle, and she taught at alternative schools in the Puget Sound region. Kimberly has extensive training in non-violent communication and conflict resolution. Her love of nature, writing, teaching, gardening, herbs, fantasy books and storytelling led her to create Herb Fairies.

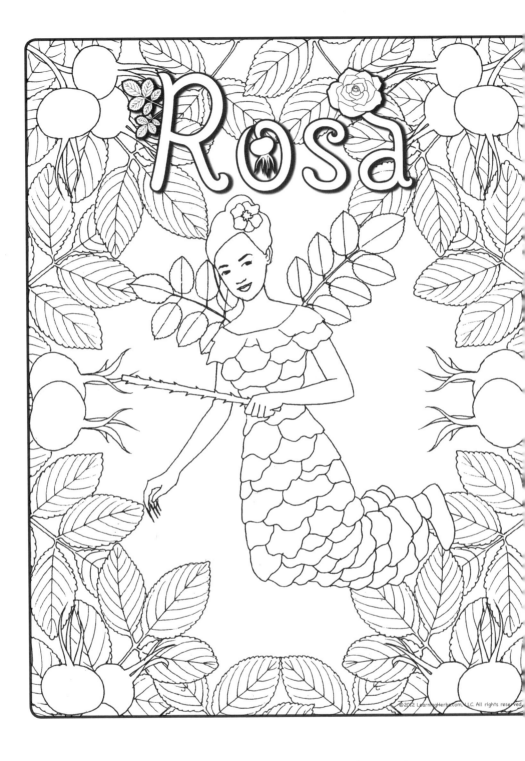

Download Herb Fairies coloring pages in the member area.

Not a member? Visit HerbFairies.com.